OLIVIA™
Dances for Joy

DISCARDED

Adapted by Natalie Shaw
Based on the screenplay written by Madellaine Paxson
Illustrated by Patrick Spaziante

Based on the TV series OLIVIA™ as seen on Nickelodeon™

SIMON SPOTLIGHT
An imprint of Simon & Schuster Children's Publishing Division
New York   London   Toronto   Sydney   New Delhi
1230 Avenue of the Americas, New York, New York 10020
This Simon Spotlight paperback edition December 2016
OLIVIA™ Ian Falconer Ink Unlimited, Inc. and © 2012 Ian Falconer and Classic Media, LLC. Also available in a Simon Spotlight
deluxe storybook edition. All rights reserved, including the right of reproduction in whole or in part in any form. SIMON SPOTLIGHT and
colophon are registered trademarks of Simon & Schuster, Inc. For information about special discounts for bulk purchases, please contact
Simon & Schuster Special Sales at 1-866-506-1949 or business@simonandschuster.com.
Manufactured in the United States of America 1116 LAK   10 9 8 7 6 5 4 3 2 1
ISBN 978-1-4814-8105-2 (pbk)   •   ISBN 978-1-4424-5258-9 (eBook)

Olivia and her friends were having a great time in Grandma's dance class, as always.

"Show me your happy dance, everyone!" Grandma said. Each of the kids danced across the room, doing their favorite moves.

Ian did the "Robot," Julian did the "Moonwalk," and Olivia did lots of pirouettes.

After everyone had a turn to dance, Olivia noticed a new poster on the wall. "Who are the dancers in that poster?" she asked Grandma. "They sure look like they're having fun!"

"They're The Prancer Dancers! They won last year's Maywood Dance Contest," explained Grandma.
"We should enter this year's contest!" said Olivia. "Maybe we can get our pictures on a poster too!"
"But . . . but . . . that contest looks so hard and . . . well, just hard!" Francine said.
Olivia was already thinking about what it would be like. She smiled and said to herself, "I wonder . . ."

Olivia imagined they had just won the Maywood Dance Contest.
She took a bow and posed for the paparazzi.
"Over here, Olivia!" a photographer yelled.
"Give us your famous smile!" said another.
"That's enough, fellas!" replied Olivia.
"Just one more photo," begged another. "This one is for the poster."
She blew a kiss at the photographers and posed for one last picture.
Then she heard someone calling her name. . . .

"Hello? Olivia?" Ian asked, waking his sister from her daydream. "Is anybody home?"

"Sorry, I was just thinking about what it would be like to win the dance contest," Olivia said.

"We don't have a chance. The Prancer Dancers always win," Francine insisted, pointing at the team on the poster. "They dance perfectly together all the time."

"That doesn't sound like much fun!" replied Olivia. "How good can those Dancy Prancers be, anyway?"
"They're called The Prancer Dancers, and you can all see them for yourselves at their rehearsal tomorrow," answered Daisy.

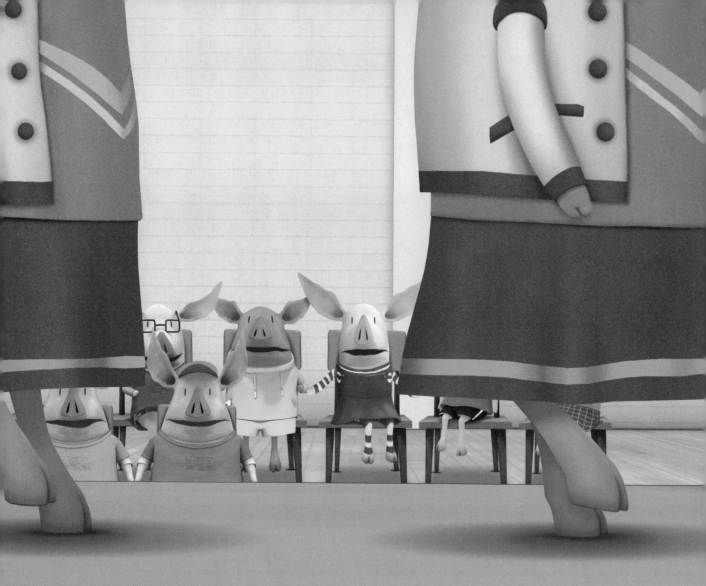

The next day at the rehearsal, The Prancer Dancers lived up to their reputation. They did exactly the same dance moves at exactly the same time. They were perfect. When they were finished, Ian started to clap, until he saw Olivia glaring at him. "We're going to get stomped," Otto said. "Sorry, Olivia, but we don't want to lose." He walked out of the room, and Oscar and Alexandra followed him.

Daisy was about to leave too, but Olivia begged her to stay.

"There's nothing you can do to make me stay on the team—" Daisy said.

"What if I name the team 'Daisy's Dancers'?" Olivia interrupted.

"Except that," Daisy finished. "Count me in! But we need nine dancers to enter the contest. Where will we find three more dancers?"

Olivia set off to find more dancers. Suddenly she spotted the mailman running away from a tiny, barking dog. But he wasn't running, exactly. He was zigging and zagging.

"Ha, ha! You think you can catch me?" the mailman shouted, zigzagging and spinning away as the little dog tried to keep up.

"That's one dancer," Olivia said to herself.

Soon after, Olivia heard someone beat-boxing.
It was Firefighter Fred.
"Oh yeah! Uh-huh!" Firefighter Fred rapped as
he polished the fire truck, pausing to pop and lock.
"That's the second dancer!" Olivia said.

Next Olivia walked by school and heard a bell ringing. She looked through the classroom window and saw Mrs. Hoggenmuller ringing a cowbell, singing, shimmying, and doing the Locomotion for her live audience . . . the class pets! "Chugga, chugga, chugga, chugga . . . Choo! Choo!" Mrs. Hoggenmuller said. "That's the third dancer!" Olivia said, and went inside to ask Mrs. Hoggenmuller to join the team.

Now that there were nine dancers on the Daisy's Dancers team, it was time for the first rehearsal. Daisy tried to teach everyone to do a perfect ballet twirl. Everyone tried to follow along, but Mrs. Hoggenmuller kept doing the Locomotion by mistake and Julian kept bumping into everyone.
"Try not to look so wobbly," said Daisy. "Spin, people!"

Julian tried to spin faster but became so dizzy that he spun out of control and knocked everyone to the ground.

"This is hopeless! None of you can dance alike." Daisy pouted. "Sorry, Olivia, but I quit!"

Grandma had been watching the rehearsal and asked Olivia what was wrong.

"Julian can't spin," Olivia said.

"But he can do the Moonwalk,"
Grandma replied.

"But Francine can't do the Moonwalk.
She can only tap dance," explained Olivia.

"We can all dance, but we can't dance
the same way. We'll never win."

"Maybe you should try to forget about winning and just dance because it makes you happy!" said Grandma. "Dance for joy!"
"That's it!" Olivia said. She asked Grandma to take Daisy's spot and gave the team a new name: The Joy Dancers!

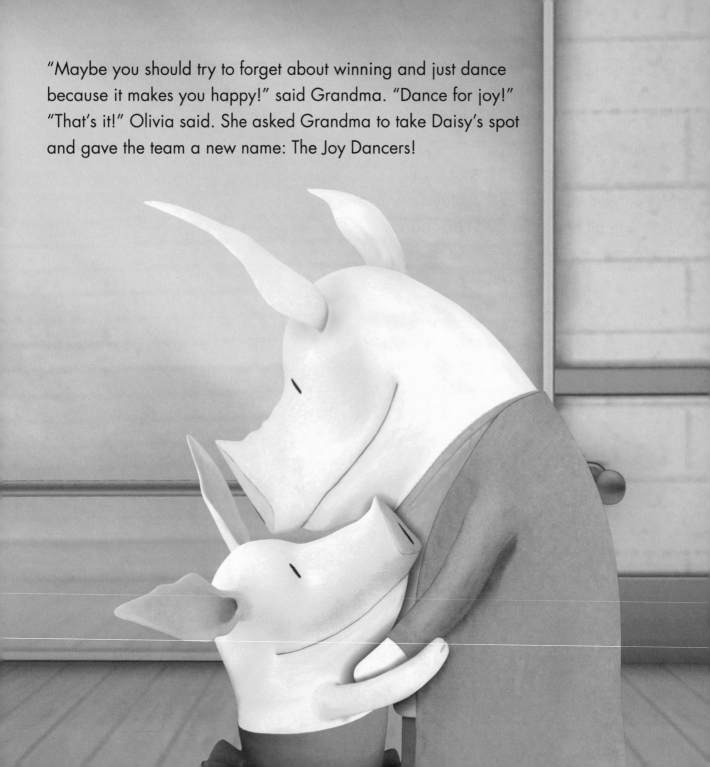

Finally, it was the night of the big contest. After The Prancer Dancers did their famous dance, it was time for Olivia's team to go.

"We have a new team this year," said the announcer. "Please give a warm welcome to . . . The Joy Dancers."

"Whatever you do, forget about dancing alike. Dance your happiest happy dance ever! And don't forget to have fun!" Olivia whispered to the team.

The music started and Olivia tapped Ian on the shoulder.
"Go robot, go robot, go robot," she chanted, clapping her hands and motioning for
the rest of the team to join in. Ian did his best robot dance and the crowd went wild!
"Go tapper, go tapper, go tapper," the team chanted together, and Francine
tap-danced across the stage, click-clacking her feet in time to the music.

One by one, the rest of the group
did their favorite dances.

Julian did the Moonwalk.

Harold did a country-western dance.

Mrs. Hoggenmuller did the Locomotion.

The mailman zigzagged across the stage.

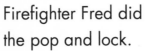

Firefighter Fred did the pop and lock.

Grandma danced the steps from her favorite ballet.

Olivia delivered a showstopping finale, doing pirouette after pirouette until the crowd rose to its feet and began to cheer! The Joy Dancers won the contest!
"Come on, Joy Dancers! Smile for the cameras!" Olivia told the team. Daisy even came by to congratulate them.

That night Grandma tucked Olivia into bed. "You really did it!"
Grandma said. "You won the contest!"
"You know what, Grandma? I'm happy we won, but I'm even
happier that we had fun!" Olivia replied sleepily.
"Good night, my happy little dancer," Grandma whispered.
Olivia fell asleep and dreamed about dancing for joy.